The Intimacy of Love

Candy LaFlora

Love—real love—is more than just a feeling or a fairytale. It's a decision, a daily pursuit, and a divine reflection. After being married for 42 years ourselves, we've come to learn that love God's way is intentional, passionate, sacrificial, and anchored in truth.

The Intimacy of Love is not just another book on marriage. It's a heart-to-heart conversation wrapped in wisdom, transparency, and the Word. Pastor Candy opens the door wide and lets us in—not into a perfect story, but into a powerful one. One built on covenant, strengthened by challenges, and centered on Christ.

We've had the privilege of knowing Pastors Stephen and Candy LaFlora, and their love is the real deal. It's steady. It's joyful. And it speaks volumes even when they say nothing at all. Their marriage is a living testimony that intimacy—spiritual, emotional, and physical—is not only possible in marriage but necessary.

Whether you're dating, engaged, newly married, or decades in like us, this book is a gift. It will stretch you, stir you, and spark something fresh in your relationship. Pastor Candy writes like a trusted friend and teaches like a seasoned leader. Every chapter is soaked in grace, full of God, and grounded in truth.

So lean in. Let the La Floras' story inspire your own. And let God breathe new life into your love.

Get ready—this book is about to pull you closer to your spouse and even closer to the One who authored love in the first place.

With all our love,
Mike & DeeDee Freeman

Dedication

To our Heavenly Father,

Thank You for giving us the blueprint and the grace to live a life rooted in love. Your Word is our guide, and Your Spirit our strength.

To my beloved husband, Stephen LaFlora—

For 39 beautiful years, you have been my partner, my covering, and my joy. Life with you is both adventurous and sweet. Thank you for loving me so well.

In loving memory of my parents,

Pastor Chester & Beatrice Dickerson Sr.

You gave me a front-row seat to what a godly, enduring marriage looks like. Your love and unity were a living example of walking in harmony for over 50 years. Your legacy lives on in me.

With all my heart,

Candy LaFlora

"When you choose to love your spouse, you're not just giving your heart—you're sharing your dreams, your laughter, your prayers, and your purpose. Real love says, 'Let's walk this road together, hand in hand, through every season.'"

— Candy LaFlora

Table of Contents

"True love doesn't fade with time—it grows deeper with every trial, every triumph, and every tear. When rooted in God, love becomes eternal—an unbreakable bond that outlives even the passing of years."

— Candy LaFlora

Foreword

The Intimacy of Love by our dear friend Candy LaFlora is a refreshing, Spirit-filled reminder of God's original and beautiful design for intimacy within marriage.

Marriage was never meant to be merely endured; it was meant to reflect the love Christ has for His Church—faithful, passionate, selfless, and eternal. This book doesn't shy away from the real challenges that couples face. Candy addresses each obstacle with biblical truth and practical hope.

As you read through chapters like *Reigniting the Spark* and *Continue to Invest in Your Marriage*, you'll be reminded that love is more than a moment—it is a daily decision, a divine commitment, and a gift meant to grow deeper with time.

Whether you're newly married, walking through a season of struggle, or simply desiring to deepen the connection with your spouse, *The Intimacy of Love* is for you. May it bless you, challenge you, and draw you closer—not just to one another, but to the God who created intimacy in the first place.

With love and great expectation,
Mark and Trina Hankins

Introduction

MARRIAGE IS ONE OF THE most sacred gifts God has given us. It is not merely a partnership or a contract—it is a divine covenant, established to reflect the love of Christ for His Church (Ephesians 5:25). And at the heart of that covenant is *intimacy*—a deep, God-designed connection that goes far beyond physical affection.

The intimacy of love involves emotional openness, spiritual unity, mutual trust, and yes, physical closeness—all grounded in a foundation of unconditional love. When true intimacy is present, it brings strength, healing, joy, and resilience into a marriage. It is a bond that reflects the very heart of God.

Unfortunately, many couples lose sight of this kind of intimacy. Life becomes busy. Stress takes center stage. Communication gets strained. Responsibilities begin to outweigh relationship. And in the process, the fun, laughter, and connection that once felt effortless can slowly fade.

But marriage was never meant to be dry or distant. It was created by God to be joyful, fulfilling, passionate, and enduring. Jesus reminds us in Matthew 18:3:

"Unless you change and become like little children, you will never enter the kingdom of heaven."

A childlike heart is full of joy, wonder, playfulness, and trust—qualities that should still live and breathe in your marriage. When couples allow themselves to be lighthearted, to laugh, and to truly enjoy each other, intimacy is revived, and love is strengthened.

In this book, we will explore what God's Word says about love, marriage, and intimacy. Together, we'll discover:

- God's original design for intimacy in marriage

- The power of emotional vulnerability and spiritual unity

- How to embrace physical intimacy as a sacred and joyful gift

- The importance of open communication and mutual respect

- How the Holy Spirit acts as the glue that bonds you together

- Why you must celebrate your differences—not try to change them

- And how to keep your marriage fun, fresh, and full of life

This book is meant to encourage, inspire, and challenge you to grow deeper in love—*not just with each other, but with God at the center of it all.*

To take it even further, I've also created The Intimacy of Love Workbook—a fun, interactive resource for couples to reflect, laugh, talk, and grow stronger together. Whether you've been married five months or fifty years, this book and workbook are tools to help you build a relationship that is full of passion, peace, and purpose.

Marriage is a journey. Intimacy is a process. But with God as your guide, you can build something that lasts a lifetime—and enjoy every moment along the way.

So come close, lean in, and let's rediscover *The Intimacy of Love.*

*"Love endures long
and is patient and kind;
love never is envious nor boils
over with jealousy, is not boastful
or vainglorious, does not
display itself haughtily.*

1 Corinthians 13:4

"*Intimacy is more than a physical connection—it's about being fully known and still fully loved. It's about building a bond so strong that life's storms can't break it and daily routine can't dull it.*"

1

God's Design for Intimacy in Marriage

When God created marriage, He didn't just think of two people living under the same roof, sharing bills and raising children. He envisioned something deeper, richer, and more beautiful—a relationship full of trust, joy, vulnerability, laughter, partnership, and passion. In other words, intimacy.

And not just the kind of intimacy we hear about in popular culture, but the kind that is rooted in God's heart and modeled in His Word. Intimacy is more than a physical connection—it's about being fully known and still fully loved. It's about building a bond so strong that life's storms can't break it and daily routine can't dull it.

Let's begin this journey by exploring the blueprint God gave us for intimacy in marriage.

Marriage as a Covenant, Not Just a Contract

Genesis 2:24 (NKJV)
"Therefore, a man shall leave his father and mother and be joined to his wife, and they shall become one flesh."

Marriage is not just a social agreement or legal contract—it's a divine covenant. It's a promise made before God to become one. Not just one in body, but in heart, purpose, spirit, and mission.

When we view marriage as a contract, we begin to treat it as something based on performance: *"If you do your part, I'll do mine."* But when we see it as a covenant, the motivation changes. It becomes: *"I'm all in—through joy and pain, ease and effort, celebration and challenge—because I made a promise to love you, and God is at the center of it."*

Covenant thinking creates a safe space for intimacy to grow. Why? Because when you know your spouse is committed for life, you're more likely to let your guard down, to open up, and to build a love that lasts.

Love as the Foundation of Intimacy

1 Corinthians 13:4-7 (NIV)
"Love is patient, love is kind. It does not envy, it does not boast, it is not proud... It always protects, always trusts, always hopes, always perseveres."

You can't build intimacy without love—*real*, godly love. Not the kind based on feelings, but the kind that shows up day after day, even when it's not easy.

Love is the foundation that holds your marriage steady when emotions waver or expectations aren't met. It's love that says, *"Even when we're not seeing eye to eye, I still choose you."*

It's patient in the morning when one of you needs three cups of coffee just to smile.

It's kind in the evening when one of you is exhausted and quiet.

It's forgiving after a misunderstanding.

And it's strong enough to cover the seasons of change that every marriage walks through.

When love is the foundation, intimacy becomes natural. You feel safe, seen, and supported—and that opens the door for deeper emotional and spiritual connection.

Physical Intimacy as a Gift from God

Song of Solomon 4:10 (NIV)
"How delightful is your love, my sister, my bride! How much more pleasing is your love than wine, and the fragrance of your perfume more than any spice!"

Let's talk about physical intimacy—and yes, let's smile while we do it! God created it, He blessed it, and He called it very good—*within the covenant of marriage.*

It's not just about sex—it's about *connection, joy,* and *oneness.* It's a form of communication, a celebration of closeness, and a powerful way to say, *"I choose you, again and again."*

Unfortunately, too many couples fall into two extremes: either they avoid the topic altogether, or they treat it like a task to check off the list. But God meant for it to be joyful, playful, and fulfilling—a place of laughter, vulnerability, and delight.

Let's Make This Real:

Imagine this: You're both tired. Dinner is done, dishes are stacked, and the day has been long. One of you makes a silly comment, the other grins. Before you know it, you're laughing like teenagers in the kitchen. There's a spark there—not forced, not planned, just real connection. That's intimacy in motion. That's where affection is born—not just in the bedroom, but in the rhythm of everyday life.

NOTE: *"Put a little Everyday in your Romance — Put a little Romance in your Everyday!"*

Physical intimacy is nurtured by emotional warmth and playful connection. So send that flirty text during the day. Steal that kiss in the hallway. Dance in the living room to your favorite love song. These small moments build a rhythm of romance that keeps your hearts close and your passion alive.

Intimacy is never supposed to be a burden. It's a blessing—a sacred way to give, receive, and rejoice in love.

Closing Thoughts

God designed marriage to be more than just surviving—it's meant to be thriving. He created you to be known, loved, and connected in every way—spiritually, emotionally, and physically.

When you embrace marriage as a covenant, build it on love, and celebrate physical intimacy as a gift, you'll discover that intimacy is not something you chase—it becomes something you live.

In the chapters to come, we'll explore even more ways to grow in love, laugh together, and let the Holy Spirit guide every part of your relationship. But for now, remember this:

Intimacy starts with God. It grows with intentionality. And it flourishes when joy, love, and grace are allowed to flow freely.

Closing Prayer:

Father God, thank You for designing marriage as a beautiful covenant between two people who are called to love, serve, and grow together. Help us to honor our marriage as a sacred promise, not just a partnership. Teach us to love one another with the selfless, enduring love that mirrors Christ's love for the Church. Let intimacy flow from emotional closeness, spiritual unity, and joyful physical connection. Restore what's been strained and deepen what's already strong. We receive Your wisdom, and we invite Your presence into every part of our relationship.

In Jesus' name, Amen.

"Vulnerability is not weakness;
it's strength wrapped in honesty."

2

Key Aspects of Intimacy in Marriage

Building a Deeper Bond Through Vulnerability, Communication, and Connection

INTIMACY IN MARRIAGE DOESN'T JUST "happen." It must be cultivated. It grows in the soil of trust, in the warmth of open hearts, and in the light of mutual respect and love.

In this chapter, we're going to take a closer look at five essential ingredients that keep intimacy alive and thriving. These qualities don't just create a stronger marriage—they create a deeper friendship, a richer partnership, and a love that can weather every season.

1. Emotional Vulnerability – Letting Down the Walls

James 5:16 (KJV)
"Confess your faults one to another, and pray one for another, that ye may be healed."

Emotional vulnerability is the gateway to intimacy. It's the willingness to let your spouse see *the real you*—the one behind the roles, the titles, and the masks. It means saying, *"This is what I'm feeling. This is where I'm struggling. This is where I need you."*

For many couples, emotional vulnerability doesn't come naturally—especially if one or both partners grew up in homes where emotions weren't welcomed or were seen as weakness. But vulnerability is not weakness; it's *strength wrapped in honesty.*

When we open our hearts, even a little, we invite our spouse into the deeper places of who we are. And when those moments are handled with gentleness and grace, trust is built, healing happens, and intimacy deepens.

A Word to the Men

Brothers, this one's for you.

Most women were designed by God to be expressive. They talk. They process. They share their hearts. And most of the time, they're *waiting on you* to do the same.

But here's the challenge: many men were taught—directly or indirectly—that showing emotion makes you soft, or that being vulnerable is somehow "less manly." Nothing could be further from the truth.

Being vulnerable with your wife doesn't make you weak—it makes you brave. It's brave to say, *"I'm overwhelmed right now."* It's courageous to say, *"I'm afraid I might fail."* It's mature to say, *"I need prayer."*

Your wife isn't your opponent—she's your greatest ally. She's got your back and your heart. But she can't stand in the gap for what you don't reveal.

Let her in. Trust her with your heart. Not just your strength—but also your struggle.

Don't let pride keep you silent. Because silence builds walls. But vulnerability builds bridges. And God can walk across those bridges to do something beautiful in your marriage.

A Note to the Women

Ladies let's talk for a moment—just us.

When your husband opens his heart, *stop everything* and listen.

Don't multitask. Don't check your phone. Don't fold the laundry, stir the pot, or half-listen while scrolling. Give him your eyes, your ears, and your full heart.

And while you're listening, don't judge. Don't defend. Don't correct.

Please—don't roll your eyes, cross your arms, or wave your hands in frustration.

He's not giving you a script.

He's giving you a piece of his heart.

And that's holy ground.

When a man opens up, especially if it's hard for him, he's saying, *"I trust you with the part of me that the world doesn't see."* That moment isn't about being right or proving a point. It's about being present.

This is the time to tap into that beautiful, loving girlfriend energy—you remember her, right? The one who made him feel seen, understood, and admired? The one who laughed at his jokes and made him feel like a king? *Be her again.*

Because when he feels nurtured, not corrected…

When he feels safe, not shut down…

When he hears love instead of judgment…

You are building his safe place.

And he will come back to that place again and again—through life's decisions, challenges, and even his failures—because you've created a sanctuary, not a battlefield.

So when he opens up… don't fix it.

Just *hold it.*

Just *honor it.*

And watch how the intimacy between you begins to grow in ways you never imagined.

2. Open Communication – Keep the Conversation Flowing

Ephesians 4:29 (KJV)
"Let no corrupt communication proceed out of your mouth, but that which is good to the use of edifying, that it may minister grace unto the hearers."

You can't have intimacy without honest, loving communication. It's how trust is built. It's how misunderstandings are cleared up. It's how affection is expressed.

But here's the key: communication isn't just about *talking*—it's also about listening. Really listening. Not just waiting for your turn to speak but tuning in to your spouse's heart.

And when you do speak, speak life. Your words are powerful. They can either tear down or build up.

So make it a daily habit to ask questions like:

- "How are you doing—really?"

- "Is there anything you need from me today?"

- "How can I pray for you?"

Those small questions create big connections.

3. Mutual Respect and Honor – Valuing Each Other as God Does

1 Peter 3:7 (NKJV)
"Husbands, likewise, dwell with them with understanding, giving honor to the wife… as being heirs together of the grace of life, that your prayers may not be hindered."

When respect is present in a marriage, intimacy feels safe. You feel seen, heard, and valued—not dismissed or taken for granted.

Respect doesn't mean agreement in every situation. It means honoring your spouse's thoughts, emotions, and needs—even when they're different from yours.

It means not cutting each other off mid-sentence.

Not mocking each other's ideas.

Not using sarcasm to cover frustration.

Instead, it looks like listening with humility, even when you disagree. It looks like speaking with kindness, even when tensions are high. It looks like choosing empathy over ego, and serving one another out of love, not obligation.

Mutual respect says:

- *"Your voice matters here."*

- *"Your feelings are valid, even if they're different from mine."*

- *"I may not understand it fully, but I will honor it because it matters to you."*

When both husband and wife commit to honoring each other—not just in public, but especially in private—the marriage becomes a place of dignity and strength.

And as 1 Peter 3:7 reminds us, this level of honor and understanding doesn't just bless your relationship—it affects your prayers. When we treat our spouse with honor, we're aligning ourselves with God's heart, and He takes notice.

In other words: Heaven backs a marriage built on respect.

So, let your words carry honor. Let your actions show value. And let your love be filled with the kind of respect that makes your spouse feel safe, supported, and sacredly seen.

4. Physical Connection Beyond the Bedroom – Intimacy in the Everyday

Song of Solomon 1:2 (NKJV)
"Let him kiss me with the kisses of his mouth—For your love is better than wine."

Intimacy doesn't begin in the bedroom. It starts in the kitchen, the hallway, the car ride, the shared laugh, the lingering hug, and the gentle glance that says, *"I still choose you."*

Physical connection is a daily rhythm. It's the touch on the shoulder as you walk past, the way you lean into each other on the couch, the warmth of your hand in theirs while praying together. These small moments are not "extra"—they are essential.

Affection isn't always about romance. Sometimes it's about reassurance. Sometimes it's about fun. And other times, it's simply a reminder: *"I'm still here. I still love you. And I still like being close to you."*

Try This:

Make it a point to add one new touchpoint each day.

- A hug that lingers.

- A kiss before you leave the room—not just the house.

- A hand resting on their leg during dinner.

- A random shoulder squeeze or back rub.

These gestures speak to the heart in a language deeper than words. They whisper, *"You're safe. You're seen. And I still want you."*

When physical connection flows naturally throughout the day, it draws you closer in every other area of intimacy as well.

5. Shared Spirituality and Purpose – Growing Together in God

Ecclesiastes 4:12 (NIV)
"Though one may be overpowered, two can defend themselves. A cord of three strands is not quickly broken."

One of the most intimate things a couple can do is pursue God together.

Praying together. Worshiping together. Studying the Word together. Serving others as a team. These aren't just spiritual practices—they're intimacy builders.

Why? Because when your spirits are aligned with God, your hearts draw closer to one another.

Shared spirituality gives your marriage depth, direction, and divine strength. It reminds you that you're not just building a life for yourselves—you're building a legacy for His Kingdom.

Try This:

- Start or end the day with a simple prayer together.

- Share what God is speaking to you personally during your quiet time.

- Attend a Bible study or small group together.

- Set a spiritual goal as a couple—like reading through a book of the Bible or memorizing Scripture together.

The more you make room for God's presence, the stronger your marriage will be.

Closing Thoughts

These five aspects—emotional vulnerability, open communication, mutual respect, physical connection, and shared spirituality—are like the fingers of ones hand. Individually, they're important. But together, they're powerful. They allow your marriage to reach, hold, comfort, protect, and bless.

Don't rush this process.

Build it daily.

Water it with prayer.

Protect it with gentleness.

And enjoy it with laughter.

Your marriage was never meant to be dry and distant. It was designed by God to be deep, close, joyful, and full of life.

And intimacy—true intimacy—is the heart of it all.

Closing Prayer:

Lord, we thank You for the gift of intimacy and the daily opportunities to build it through vulnerability, communication, and respect. Help us to open our hearts to one another with honesty and grace. Teach us to listen without judgment and to speak words that uplift and not tear down. Let our affection be consistent, and our respect be mutual. Draw us closer together spiritually, emotionally, and physically, and let our love reflect Your heart more each day. Holy Spirit, help us create a home where both hearts are safe and fully known. In Jesus' name, Amen.

Forgiveness doesn't mean forgetting or
pretending something didn't hurt.
It means releasing your right to stay
angry and inviting God to heal
what was broken.

3

Obstacles to Intimacy and How to Overcome Them

Removing the Weeds So Your Love Can Grow

EVERY MARRIAGE FACES OBSTACLES. EVEN the most loving, godly couples will hit seasons where connection feels strained and closeness feels like work. It doesn't mean something is broken—it simply means it's time to tend to the garden.

Intimacy, like a garden, requires attention. If it's neglected, weeds will grow: old wounds, busyness, assumptions, distance. But the good news is this—you can pull the weeds out. You can clear the ground. You can plant fresh seeds of love and water them with grace.

Let's walk through three common obstacles that hinder intimacy—and how to move past them with purpose, humility, and joy.

1. Unforgiveness and Past Hurts

Colossians 3:13 (NIV)
"Bear with each other and forgive one another if any of you has a grievance against someone. Forgive as the Lord forgave you."

Nothing suffocates intimacy faster than unforgiveness. You can be in the same room, same bed, same routine—but when resentment is living in your heart, closeness disappears.

Forgiveness doesn't mean forgetting or pretending something didn't hurt. It means releasing your right to stay angry and inviting God to heal what was broken. It's not about letting your spouse "off the hook"—it's about getting free yourself so love can flow again.

And forgiveness isn't just for the big betrayals. Sometimes it's the small, daily disappointments—the snappy comment, the missed cue, the failure to notice what mattered to you.

Those things may seem small, but if left unchecked, they can build silent walls. That's why the Word tells us to forgive *as the Lord forgave us.* That's a big calling—but it's also a beautiful one.

Forgiveness makes intimacy possible. It clears the air so hearts can draw close again.

2. Busyness and Distractions

Luke 10:41–42 (NIV)
"Martha, Martha," the Lord answered, "you are worried and upset about many things, but few things are needed—or indeed only one. Mary has chosen what is better..."

Let's be honest—life is full. Between work, ministry, kids, responsibilities, and even serving others, it's easy to put marriage on autopilot. You love each other, you're doing all the "right" things, but the intimacy starts to fade... not because anything is wrong—but because you're just busy.

But love doesn't thrive in the margins. Intimacy needs time.

Not just leftover time. Intentional time. Sacred time. Priority time.

Sometimes, like Martha, we're so busy *doing* that we forget to simply *be present.* But Jesus gently reminded her—and us—that the better portion is found in slowing down and sitting close.

So what does that look like practically?

- Saying "no" to one more meeting so you can say "yes" to an evening walk.

- Choosing conversation over screen time.

- Putting the phone down and picking your spouse's heart up.

Your marriage deserves undistracted attention. And when you give it, intimacy starts to bloom again.

3. Lack of Intentionality

Proverbs 5:18–19 (NKJV)
"Let your fountain be blessed, and rejoice with the wife of your youth… and always be enraptured with her love."

Marriage doesn't stay strong by accident. It grows because you keep showing up, investing, pouring in. Intimacy thrives when we treat it like something worth pursuing—again and again.

Sometimes the obstacle isn't a big conflict or even a packed schedule. It's just coasting. Getting comfortable. Losing the spark because you're doing life *next to* each other, but not *with* each other.

That's where intentionality comes in.

- Date nights: not optional—essential.

- Deep conversations: not just about bills and schedules, but *dreams, fears, hopes, and laughs.*

- Little gifts: yes, even those count! (Go ahead, surprise them with their favorite treat or a handwritten note!)

Remember the joy of pursuit? The butterflies? The effort you made to learn what made your spouse smile? That doesn't have to disappear. You can reignite it—on purpose.

And here's a secret: when you're intentional, the small things become big again.

A compliment lands deeper.

A touch lingers longer.

A moment feels sacred.

Because love—when tended to—is always ready to grow.

Closing Thoughts

Obstacles in marriage don't have to be permanent. When you recognize what's standing in the way of intimacy, and take intentional steps to remove it, you're making room for something far more beautiful: *deeper love, lasting closeness, and a marriage that reflects the heart of God.*

Let's be couples who forgive quickly, slow down often, and pursue each other intentionally. Because a flourishing marriage isn't just about avoiding what breaks it—

—it's about choosing daily what builds it.

Closing Prayer:

Father, we surrender every obstacle that has tried to come between us—past hurts, unforgiveness, distractions, and the times we've failed to be intentional. Heal the wounds we've held onto. Help us to forgive freely and to make time for one another again. Reignite our desire to pursue each other with fresh eyes and renewed joy. Show us how to prioritize what matters and release what doesn't. Let nothing come between the love You've given us. Restore, refresh, and strengthen the intimacy in our marriage.

In Jesus' name, Amen.

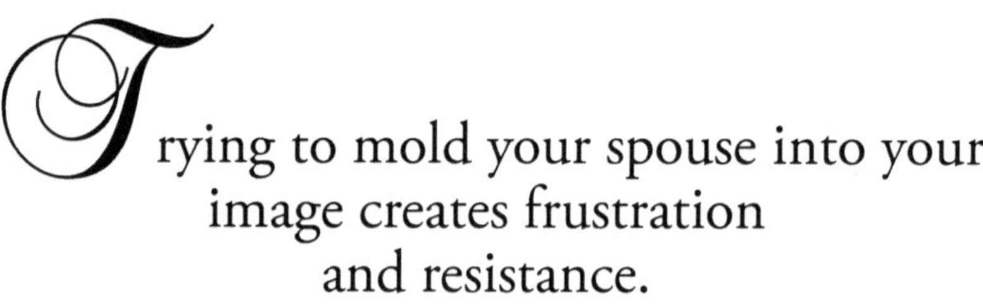

Trying to mold your spouse into your
image creates frustration
and resistance.

4

Don't Try to Conform—Celebrate!

Embracing Your Spouse's Uniqueness in Marriage

IN MARRIAGE, IT'S EASY TO slip into the habit of wanting your spouse to be more like you. Maybe you think, *"If they just thought like I did… if they handled things the way I do… if they were a little more (fill in the blank), life would be easier."*

But here's the truth: God didn't give you a clone—He gave you a complement.

He joined you with someone uniquely designed to bring balance, challenge, growth, and strength into your life. Your spouse is different from you on purpose, *and for purpose.*

Trying to mold your spouse into your image creates frustration and resistance. But when you learn to celebrate their uniqueness, you unlock a deeper level of connection, joy, and appreciation. Marriage isn't about sameness—it's about sacred synergy.

I. Biblical Foundation: God's Design for Uniqueness in Marriage

1. God Created Us Wonderfully Unique

Psalm 139:14
*"I praise You because I am fearfully and wonderfully made;
Your works are wonderful, I know that full well."*

Each spouse comes into the marriage with different personalities, backgrounds, temperaments, and ways of thinking. And that's not a problem—it's part of God's plan.

You are not supposed to think exactly alike, process emotion the same way, or solve every issue identically. Instead, you are meant to value and honor the uniqueness God placed in each other.

2. Marriage Is a Union of Differences, Not Sameness

Genesis 2:18
"The Lord God said, 'It is not good for the man to be alone. I will make a helper suitable for him.'"

God didn't create Eve to be Adam's copy—He created her to complement him. To bring what he didn't have. To complete the picture of partnership. Your marriage is not about *mirror images*; it's about intertwined strengths.

3. Unity Does Not Mean Uniformity

Romans 12:4–6
"For just as each of us has one body with many members... we have different gifts, according to the grace given to each of us."

In the body of Christ—and in the covenant of marriage—each part plays a vital role. A hand isn't less important than an eye just because it functions differently. When we embrace the truth that unity allows for differences, we stop competing and start completing each other.

II. Why We Try to Change Our Spouse (and Why We Shouldn't!)

Let's be honest—it's tempting to try to change each other. But often, it comes from the wrong place:

- Expectations from upbringing: You may be trying to replicate what you saw modeled as "normal" or "ideal."

- Desire for control: It's easier when people see things your way. But control is not connection.

- Frustration with differences: What we don't understand, we tend to resist.

- Unrealistic comparisons: Social media or other marriages may paint a picture that leads to discontent.

But Scripture gives us a better perspective:

Proverbs 27:17
"As iron sharpens iron, so one person sharpens another."

Your spouse isn't in your life to become you. They are in your life to sharpen you—to help you grow, stretch, and become more Christlike. The friction that comes from your differences? That's what sharpens your marriage and makes it strong.

III. Celebrate Your Differences: How to Appreciate Your Spouse

1. Recognize That Your Spouse Complements You

Ecclesiastes 4:9-10

"Two are better than one… If either of them falls down, one can help the other up."

Your strengths cover their weaknesses—and their strengths cover yours. That's God's design. Rather than fighting the difference, learn to lean into it.

2. Learn from Their Perspective

Instead of resisting your spouse's different way of thinking, get curious. Ask them to explain how they see things, and listen with the goal of understanding, not correcting.

3. Express Gratitude for Their Unique Qualities

Let them know what you love about their difference. Say it out loud. Often.

Example: *"I love how calm you are when I feel overwhelmed. It helps me find peace too."*

4. Use Differences to Strengthen Your Relationship

Let your spouse's uniqueness help grow you. If they're patient and you're fast-paced, let their calmness teach you peace. If you're expressive and they're reserved, let your joy bring color to their world.

IV. Practical Ways to Celebrate Your Spouse

- The "Celebrate You" Exercise

Write down 3 things you admire about your spouse's differences. Share them aloud with a smile and a grateful heart.

- Switch Roles for a Day

Try stepping into each other's shoes—it builds compassion and admiration.

- Speak Their Love Language

Discover what makes them feel most loved—and do that, even if it's not your natural go-to.

- Create a "We Balance Each Other" List

Together, write down how your differences make you stronger. You'll be surprised at how much God has blended you to build each other up.

V. The Bigger Picture: Marriage as a Reflection of Christ

Ephesians 5:25
"Husbands, love your wives, just as Christ loved the church and gave himself up for her."

Christ didn't love us because we were just like Him—He loved us in our weakness, in our uniqueness, and with full acceptance. Your marriage should reflect that kind of love.

When we celebrate each other instead of trying to change each other, we reflect the heart of Christ.

Conclusion & Reflection Questions

Let's reflect:

1. What is one difference between you and your spouse that *used to* frustrate you, but now you've come to appreciate?

2. How can you celebrate your spouse's uniqueness this week in a practical way?

3. What unique strength does your spouse bring to your life that you may be overlooking?

Closing Prayer:

Lord, thank You for creating each of us uniquely. Help us to celebrate and appreciate the differences in our marriage, seeing them as strengths rather than weaknesses. Teach us to love one another as You love us—with grace, patience, and joy. In Jesus' name, Amen.

It is not conceited (arrogant and inflated with pride); it is not rude (unmannerly) and does not act unbecomingly. Love (God's love in us) does not insist on its own rights or its own way, for it is not self-seeking; it is not touchy or fretful or resentful; it takes no account of the evil done to it [it pays no attention to a suffered wrong].

1 Corinthians 13:5

He will guide you through
conflict and lead you back
into unity.

5

The Holy Spirit — Our Glue That Bonds Us Together

Listening to and Learning from the Holy Spirit's Wisdom in Marriage

MARRIAGE IS A COVENANT MADE between a husband, a wife, and God—but it's the Holy Spirit who holds everything together. He is the unseen strength, the divine whisper, the quiet guide who brings peace in conflict and unity in chaos.

Just like glue bonds two surfaces into one, the Holy Spirit bonds our hearts together in a way that is lasting and supernatural.

As Pastor Mark Hankins said so perfectly:

"The Holy Spirit is a genius! If you listen to Him, He will make you look smart."

And it's true. When we lean on His wisdom—especially in marriage—we gain insight that's beyond human reason. He helps us see what we couldn't see, say what we wouldn't say, and love how we couldn't love in our own strength.

The Holy Spirit is not a passive presence in your life. He's an active, living guide and teacher, and He wants to partner with you in every part of your marriage.

I. The Holy Spirit's Role in Your Marriage

1. The Holy Spirit is Our Helper

John 14:26
"But the Helper, the Holy Spirit, whom the Father will send in My name, He will teach you all things and bring to your remembrance all things that I said to you."

Marriage can be beautiful—but it can also be challenging. Thankfully, we have help. The Holy Spirit teaches us how to love, reminds us of truth when emotions cloud our thinking, and gently nudges us toward grace.

He gives insight into what your spouse needs—even when they're not saying it. He helps you respond with patience when your flesh wants to react. He will guide you through conflict and lead you back into unity.

2. The Holy Spirit Produces the Fruit of a Strong Marriage

Galatians 5:22–23
"But the fruit of the Spirit is love, joy, peace, forbearance, kindness, goodness, faithfulness, gentleness and self-control."

Every one of those fruits is a marriage builder. When you're full of the Holy Spirit, you're full of the very things that create intimacy and trust. Your home becomes a place of peace, your conversations carry kindness, and your actions are marked by self-control.

You don't have to produce these fruits in your own strength. They are the natural result of a life connected to the Spirit.

3. The Holy Spirit Brings Unity, Not Division

Ephesians 4:3
"Make every effort to keep the unity of the Spirit through the bond of peace."

Division is the enemy's plan. Unity is God's. And the Holy Spirit is the one who builds the bridge back to each other when tension tries to pull you apart.

When you feel disconnected, the Holy Spirit is the one whispering, *"Go first. Say sorry. Don't shut down. Try again."*

The more you yield to Him, the stronger your bond will grow.

II. How to Listen to the Holy Spirit in Marriage

1. Be Sensitive to His Voice

Isaiah 30:21
"Whether you turn to the right or to the left, your ears will hear a voice behind you, saying, 'This is the way; walk in it.'"

The Holy Spirit doesn't shout—He whispers. He speaks through peace, conviction, Scripture, and sometimes even through your spouse.

Ask Him: *"Holy Spirit, how do You want me to respond right now?"*

You'll be amazed at what He reveals when you simply ask.

2. Pause Before Reacting

James 1:19–20
"Everyone should be quick to listen, slow to speak and slow to become angry…"

When emotions run high, our first instinct is usually wrong. That's why pausing is powerful. It gives the Holy Spirit a chance to speak before your flesh does.

Next time something stings or irritates you, don't fire back. Pause. Breathe. Invite the Holy Spirit in.

What you say next might save a whole conversation.

3. Pray Together and Seek His Guidance

Matthew 18:19–20
"If two of you agree on earth… it will be done… For where two or three are gathered together in My name, I am there in the midst of them."

Couples that pray together make room for God's wisdom and presence. It doesn't have to be long or fancy—just sincere.

There is something powerful about hearing your spouse's heart in prayer. It softens anger. It builds trust. It reminds you that you're on the same team.

4. Let the Holy Spirit Convict Instead of Trying to Change Your Spouse

John 16:8
"When He comes, He will convict the world concerning sin and righteousness and judgment."

It's not your job to fix your spouse—it's the Holy Spirit's.

Nagging, guilt, or silent treatment won't change hearts. But prayer will.

When you pray, *"Holy Spirit, work in their heart,"* He can do more in one moment than you could do in a month of arguing.

III. Signs You Are Led by the Holy Spirit in Your Marriage

- You experience peace even in difficult situations. *(Philippians 4:7)*

- You respond with love instead of anger. *(1 Corinthians 13:5–7)*

- You feel prompted to forgive and show grace. *(Colossians 3:13)*

- You seek wisdom before making decisions. *(Proverbs 3:5–6)*

- You sense God's presence in your home. *(Psalm 127:1)*

These are the fruits of a Spirit-led marriage. And they can be yours—when you listen and yield to Him.

IV. Practical Ways to Invite the Holy Spirit into Your Marriage

1. Pray Together Daily

Even if it's just a one-minute prayer. *"Holy Spirit, guide us today."*

2. Read Scripture Together

God's Word tunes your heart to hear His voice.

3. Worship Together

Turn on worship music. Sing. Lift your hands. Let His presence fill your home.

4. Speak Life Over Each Other

Your words matter. Choose ones that echo the Spirit's heart.

5. Ask for Help Before Conflict

Before the argument begins, whisper *"Holy Spirit, help me."* That moment of surrender can change the whole direction.

V. Fun Activity: "Holy Spirit Lead Us" Challenge

Objective:

Help couples practice listening to the Holy Spirit and responding with His wisdom rather than emotion.

How to Play:

1. Each couple gets three scenario cards (or comes up with their own).

2. One person reads a scenario.

3. The other must pause, pray, and respond as they believe the Holy Spirit would guide them.

Example Scenarios:

- Your spouse forgot your birthday. You feel hurt. What do you say?

- You disagree about a parenting decision. What does love look like in that moment?

- Your spouse is overwhelmed and distant. What might the Holy Spirit prompt you to do?

Talk about it after! Share how the Spirit's wisdom often looks different from your initial feelings.

VI. Closing Thoughts & Reflection

The Holy Spirit truly is the glue in your marriage. He connects hearts, corrects attitudes, builds unity, and gives wisdom far beyond our own.

Let Him be your guide—not just in the big decisions, but in the everyday moments where intimacy is built and love is tested.

Trust Him. Listen to Him. And let Him lead you—together.

Reflection Questions

1. Can you remember a time the Holy Spirit helped you handle a difficult moment in your marriage?

2. Is there an area in your relationship where you've been leaning on your own strength instead of His?

3. What is one step you'll take this week to invite the Holy Spirit more into your marriage?

Closing Prayer

Holy Spirit, we invite You to be the center of our marriage. Teach us to listen to Your voice, to respond with love, and to walk in unity. Help us lean on Your wisdom instead of our own understanding. Let Your presence be the glue that holds us together. In Jesus' name, Amen.

It does not rejoice at injustice and unrighteousness, but rejoices when right and truth prevail.

1 Corinthians 13:6

*S*omewhere along the way, between the bills, the responsibilities, the kids, the calendar, and the never-ending "to-do" list, many couples lose their sense of play.

6

Remember—
It's Supposed to Be Fun!

Keeping Joy, Laughter, and Freedom Alive in Your Marriage

MARRIAGE ISN'T MEANT TO FEEL like a job description or a duty list. It's supposed to be fun!

Yes—*fun!* God designed marriage to be a joyful, life-giving, heart-sparking adventure shared between two people who love each other deeply and laugh together often.

Somewhere along the way, between the bills, the responsibilities, the kids, the calendar, and the never-ending "to-do" list, many couples lose their sense of *play*. They forget how to laugh. They forget how to be lighthearted. They forget that intimacy breathes best where joy lives.

But here's your reminder: you're allowed to enjoy each other.

You're allowed to be silly.

You're allowed to flirt.

You're allowed to dance in the kitchen and laugh at inside jokes until you cry.

Because a marriage full of joy is a marriage full of life.

Jesus Reminds Us to Be Childlike

Matthew 18:3
"Unless you change and become like little children, you will never enter the kingdom of heaven."

A childlike heart is full of wonder, joy, trust, and simplicity. And believe it or not, that same posture invites intimacy into your marriage.

Children forgive quickly.

They laugh easily.

They trust fully.

They live in the moment.

And when we carry that kind of lightness into our relationship, we allow walls to fall and hearts to open.

We stop overthinking. We stop holding back. We stop being so serious.

We just enjoy each other again.

How Fun Protects Intimacy

Laughter disarms conflict.

Joy relieves tension.

Playfulness reconnects what pressure pulls apart.

When you laugh together, you remember you're on the same team.

When you flirt, you reignite that spark.

When you stop taking everything so seriously, you make room for love to breathe again.

And let's be honest—marriage is hard work sometimes. But if it's *all* work and no play, something's out of balance. Let the kid in you come out. Let the joy rise up again. It's supposed to be fun!

Ways to Add Fun Back into Your Marriage

1. Laugh More on Purpose

Watch a comedy. Tell stories from your childhood. Look through old photos and remember the awkward hairstyles and matching outfits!

2. Be Playful Again

Race to the car. Play a board game. Dance in the living room. Chase each other around the house if you have to!

3. Surprise Each Other

Small surprises—like your spouse's favorite snack, a sticky note on the mirror, or a silly video—can create big connection.

4. Have Regular Date Nights

These don't need to be expensive. Take a walk, go get dessert, or sit in the backyard and dream out loud.

5. Reminisce About Your "Firsts"

Talk about the first date. The first kiss. The first time you realized, *"This is my person."* Reliving those moments brings warmth and appreciation.

Fun Activity: "Remember When…"

Set aside 10 minutes to sit together with no distractions. Take turns finishing this sentence:

"Remember when we…"

Let each memory take you back. Laugh. Smile. Relive the moment.

You'll be surprised how this simple exercise will remind you of just how much you've built together—and how much fun you've already had.

Then ask:

"What can we do this week to create a new memory?"

Closing Thoughts

Life will always be busy. But don't let the weight of "real life" crush the joy out of your relationship.

Let go. Laugh more. Be light.

God gave you each other not just to build a life—but to enjoy the ride.

So go ahead…

Laugh loud.

Flirt often.

Be goofy.

Make memories.

And remember: it's supposed to be fun.

Reflection Questions

1. What's something fun you used to do together that you've stopped doing?

2. What small way can you bring more laughter into your marriage this week?

3. What makes your spouse smile—and how can you do more of it?

Closing Prayer

Father, thank You for the joy that comes from love. Remind us to laugh more, to play more, and to stop taking life—and each other—so seriously. Breathe fresh joy into our marriage. Let our home be filled with lightness and laughter. Help us find reasons to celebrate, to dance, and to be grateful every single day. Thank You that love can be fun. Holy Spirit, make our relationship a place of peace, passion, and play.

In Jesus' name, Amen!

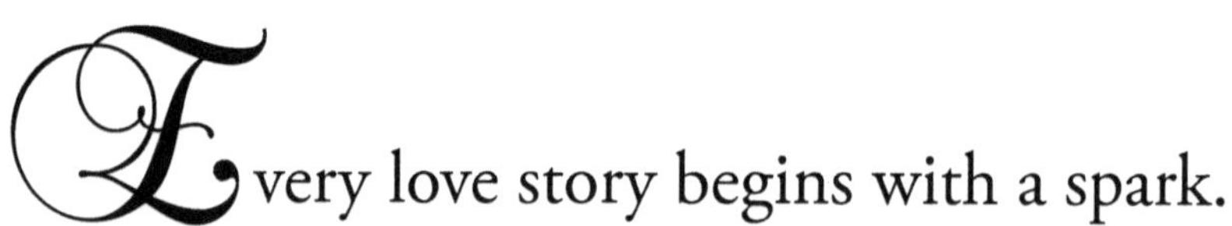

Every love story begins with a spark.

7

Reigniting the Spark

**Returning to Your First Love in Marriage
Every love story begins with a spark.**

THAT LOOK ACROSS THE ROOM. That nervous laugh. That first date where time flew by. The butterflies. The inside jokes. The phone calls that lasted hours. You couldn't wait to see each other. You dressed up for them. You left love notes. You stayed up late dreaming together.

It was sweet. Exciting. New.

And it was intentional.

But what started with passion can slowly shift into routine.

Not because the love is gone, but because life gets loud—and love, if we're not careful, can get quiet.

The spark doesn't disappear. It just hides under layers of laundry, bills, appointments, and responsibilities.

Here's the good news:

You can get it back.

In fact, God wants you to.

Revelation: A Message to the Married

In Revelation 2, Jesus speaks to the church in Ephesus. He recognizes their hard work, endurance, and faithfulness—but then He says something powerful:

Revelation 2:4–5 (NIV)
"Yet I hold this against you: You have forsaken the love you had at first. Consider how far you have fallen! Repent and do the things you did at first."

What a message.

They were doing all the right things—but they had left their first love.

And isn't that a picture of what happens in many marriages?

We're faithful. We're working hard. We're showing up.

But we've left the passionate pursuit behind.

We stopped doing the things we did at first.

And little by little, that love becomes familiar… then routine… and sometimes, *lukewarm.*

The Laodicean church in Revelation 3 was rebuked for exactly that.

Revelation 3:15–16 (NIV)
"I know your deeds, that you are neither cold nor hot… So, because you are lukewarm—neither hot nor cold—I am about to spit you out of my mouth.

Jesus wants hot love—fervent, intentional, passionate love—not just with Him, but between His people, too.

And if it matters to Jesus in our relationship with Him, it surely matters in our marriage.

How Did You Fall in Love in the First Place?

Let's take a moment. Think back to the early days of your relationship.

- What did you do that made your spouse feel cherished?

- How did you speak to them?

- What risks did you take to get their attention?

- What sacrifices did you make to show them they were worth it?

That's your blueprint.

Jesus said, "Do the things you did at first."

So if you used to write notes—write them again.

If you used to dress up—do it again.

If you used to hold hands and flirt—do it again.

If you used to look in their eyes when they spoke—start again.

Reigniting the spark doesn't always require something new.

Sometimes it just takes remembering and returning.

5 Practical Ways to Reignite the Spark

1. Schedule Uninterrupted Time Together

Turn off the phones. Put away the calendar. Just be *together*. Quality time creates connection—and connection fuels intimacy.

2. Initiate Affection, Not Just Obligation

   Let hugs, kisses, and touches be part of your daily rhythm—not just a lead-in to romance, but part of the heartbeat of your relationship.

3. Surprise One Another Again

   Spontaneity adds excitement. Plan a date. Leave a love note. Show up with their favorite treat. Show them: *"I'm still pursuing you."*

4. Talk About Dreams, Not Just Schedules

   What are you hoping for? What's God stirring in your heart? These conversations build emotional closeness and remind you that you're building something together.

5. Revisit Special Memories Together

   Look at old photos. Watch your wedding video. Revisit the place where you first met or had your first date. Let your heart go back, and your passion will follow.

Warning Signs of a Cooling Marriage

- You're always talking about logistics, not love.

- Physical intimacy feels forced or nonexistent.

- There's laughter with others, but rarely with each other.

- You can't remember the last time you were excited to see your spouse.

If that sounds familiar, don't panic.

Just pause, pray, and return.

Return to the love you had at first. Not just the feelings—but the actions that fed those feelings.

God is a Restorer of Romance

You may feel like the fire's gone. But with God, no flame is too small to rekindle.

He specializes in resurrection. And that includes your passion, romance, and joy.

It's never too late to love deeply again.

God doesn't want your marriage to survive—He wants it to thrive.

Reflection Questions

1. What are 2–3 things you used to do in the beginning of your relationship that you've stopped doing?

2. How does the message to the churches in Revelation speak to your marriage today?

3. What's one intentional step you can take this week to pursue your spouse and reignite the spark?

Closing Prayer

Father, thank You for the spark that started our love—and thank You that it can be reignited. Help us to return to our first love, not just with You, but with each other. Remind us of the joy, laughter, and passion we once shared, and teach us how to rekindle it in fresh and meaningful ways. Lord, let our love be hot—not lukewarm. Let us pursue one another with purpose and delight. Breathe new life into our connection and romance, and help us never forget the beauty of falling in love all over again.

In Jesus' name, Amen!

*Love bears up under
anything and everything that
comes, is ever ready to believe the
best of every person, its hopes are
fadeless under all circumstances,
and it endures everything
[without weakening].*

1 Corinthians 13:7

And enduring love
doesn't happen by accident. It's built.
On purpose. With prayer, patience,
forgiveness, fun, and fire.

8

Love That Endures

**Building a Marriage That Lasts
In a world where so much fades, lasting love is a treasure.**

NOT JUST THE KIND OF love that stays because of duty, but the kind that grows deeper through seasons, stronger through storms, and sweeter with time. It's the kind of love that still holds hands in old age. The kind that still says, *"You're my person,"* after all the changes life brings. It's the kind of love that *endures.*

And enduring love doesn't happen by accident.

It's built.

On purpose.

With prayer, patience, forgiveness, fun, and fire.

A Legacy of Lasting Love

I've had the rare and priceless gift of witnessing what true, enduring love looks like—up close, personal, and real—through the marriage of my parents, Pastor Chester and Beatrice Dickerson, Sr.

They were married for 50 beautiful years. Not perfect years, but years filled with faith, laughter, partnership, and deep affection. My mother was his everything—his queen, his joy, the love of his life. And when she went to heaven, part of his heart went with her.

But even in her absence, he never stopped loving her.

He kept her photo tucked in his wallet—not just out of habit, but out of devotion. He would take it out and show it proudly, with a smile in his eyes and tenderness in his voice as he called her "my beautiful bride."

He talked about her often, not with sorrow, but with a kind of reverent joy—like a man still in love. Even as the years passed, that love never faded. It never cooled. If anything, it grew deeper, richer, more sacred.

And when he went to heaven, I know he went with a full heart—ready to see his bride again.

That is the kind of love that stays.

That is the kind of love that teaches, anchors, and leaves a legacy.

Their marriage wasn't just a model—it was a ministry.

It showed me, and so many others, what it means to love with endurance, honor, faithfulness, and fire.

It was a covenant, not just a commitment. That's what enduring love looks like. It's not perfect—but it's faithful.

It weathers the seasons, and with God at the center, it becomes a testimony for generations to come. And even in death, it continued to preach the power of love that never lets go.

"Picture of 1ˢᵗ Wedding"
May 27, 1950

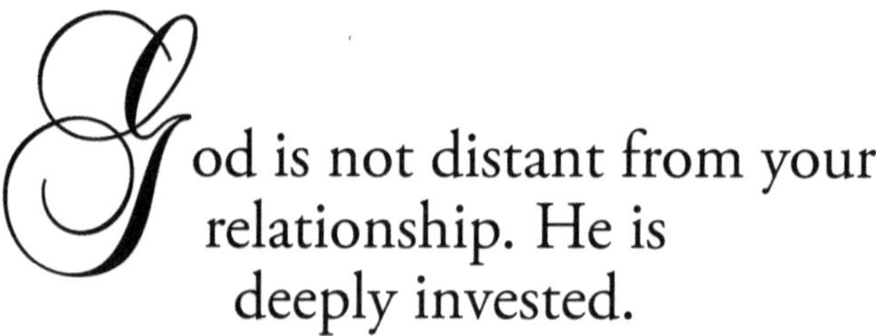God is not distant from your
relationship. He is
deeply invested.

9

A Prayer for Your Marriage

Inviting God's Blessing Over Your Relationship

YOU'VE WALKED THROUGH THE PAGES of this book.

You've laughed, reflected, remembered, and maybe even shed a few tears.

You've been challenged to grow, to forgive, to play, to pray, and to fall in love all over again.

But above all else, my prayer is that you've sensed the Father's heart for your marriage.

God is not distant from your relationship. He is deeply invested.

He created marriage. He breathed life into it.

And He desires to walk with you through every season of it.

No matter where you are right now—thriving, struggling, or somewhere in between—God is for you.

He is ready to strengthen your bond, heal what's broken, deepen your joy, and bring fresh purpose to your love.

And so, as we come to the end of this book, I want to invite you to do something simple, but powerful:

Pray. Together.

Not just read a prayer—but truly pause, hold hands if you can, and invite God's presence to rest on your home, your hearts, and your covenant.

Colossians 1:9–14 (AMP)
"For this reason, since the day we heard about it, we have not stopped praying for you—asking [specifically] that you may be filled with the knowledge of His will in all spiritual wisdom [with insight into His purposes], and in understanding [of spiritual things], so that you will walk in a manner worthy of the Lord [displaying admirable character, moral courage, and personal integrity], to fully please Him in all things, bearing fruit in every good work and steadily growing in the knowledge of God [with deeper faith, clearer insight, and fervent love for His precepts];

[We pray that you may be] strengthened and invigorated with all power, according to His glorious might, to attain every kind of endurance and patience with joy; giving thanks to the Father, who has qualified us to share in the inheritance of the saints (God's people) in the Light.

For He has rescued us and has drawn us to Himself from the dominion of darkness, and has transferred us to the kingdom of His beloved Son, in whom we have redemption [because of His sacrifice], the forgiveness of sins [and the cancellation of sins' penalty]."

A Personal Prayer for You

Father, thank You for the couple reading this right now. Thank You for the love they share, and even more, for the love You have poured out over them. I ask You to cover their marriage in grace, strength, and peace.

Let this relationship be a living example of Your covenant love—full of mercy, passion, kindness, and joy. Teach them how to walk in unity and intimacy. Let laughter echo through their home and Your presence rest in every room. Heal what's been hurt. Restore what's been strained. And bless what's been faithfully built.

Strengthen their connection—spiritually, emotionally, and physically. Make them slow to speak, quick to listen, and even quicker to forgive. Let them be a team in every season, drawing on Your wisdom and leaning into Your Spirit daily.

And Lord, may their love story never grow cold—but grow brighter with time, always returning to the first love, and reflecting the love of Jesus in every word, every touch, and every choice.

I bless their marriage in the mighty name of Jesus, and I declare that the best is still ahead. Amen.

Thank you for allowing me to walk with you through *The Intimacy of Love.*

May your marriage be everything God intended it to be—passionate, powerful, and beautifully anchored in Him.

Now, go love each other deeply. Laugh loudly. Forgive quickly. And never stop growing together.

This is only the beginning.

With all my heart,

Pastor Candy LaFlora

10

Continue to Invest in Your Marriage

"For where your treasure is, there will your heart be also."
— Matthew 6:21 (KJV)

HAVE YOU EVER NOTICED HOW we tend to nurture what we truly value? Whether it's a career, a home, a hobby—or even a favorite outfit—we put time, money, and energy into it because we care about it. We maintain it, protect it, and prioritize it.

Now pause for a moment and consider: Isn't your marriage worth even more?

The Principle of Investment

Jesus gave us a profound truth in Matthew 6:21: "For where your treasure is, there will your heart be also."

In other words, your heart follows your investments. Where you consistently give—your attention, your affection, your time, your resources—your heart naturally follows. That's why neglect can be so dangerous. Anything left unattended will eventually fall apart. That includes our marriages.

Love does not sustain itself without effort. Just as a garden must be watered, weeded, and tended, so too must a marriage be cultivated with intention and care. A strong marriage doesn't just happen—it's built over time through regular, loving investments.

Order Brings Strength

No one puts their money into a machine that has an "Out of Order" sign.

The same is true in marriage. If we're going to invest in something, it has to be in proper working order—and the best way to ensure that is to align our marriage with God's design.

When investing in your marriage, it's important to align it with the order that God has created for marriage. That means spending time meditating on what God says about love, marriage, sex, and money. When we do, we replenish our bond and begin to build a deeper, richer love than we ever thought possible.

Order is not a bad word. It's not about control or restriction. In fact, godly order brings freedom. There is liberty and ease when things operate in the flow of God's divine design. It removes chaos and invites peace. When your marriage is in order, it becomes fertile ground for love, joy, and growth.

Practical Ways to Invest

Here are just a few ways to keep sowing into the sacred bond of your marriage:

- Time — Quality time isn't a luxury; it's a necessity. Even in busy seasons, find consistent moments to connect.

- Words — Speak life into your spouse. Encourage. Compliment. Speak kindly and often.

- Prayer — Invite God into your daily life as a couple. Pray with and for each other.

- Touch — Physical affection affirms love. A warm hug, a gentle touch, a kiss hello or goodbye—these things matter.

- Generosity — Surprise one another with small gifts, acts of service, or unexpected kindness.

Marriage is not a 50/50 arrangement. It's two people giving 100%—even on days when one may only have 30% to give. Investment isn't always glamorous, but it's always worth it.

Reflection Questions

1. What have I been intentionally sowing into my marriage lately?

2. Are there areas where I've unintentionally been neglectful?

3. What's one investment I can begin making again starting today?

Suggested Scripture Reading

- Ecclesiastes 4:9-10 – "Two are better than one… for if they fall, one will lift up his companion."

- Proverbs 11:25 – "The generous soul will be made rich, and he who waters will also be watered himself."

- Galatians 6:9 – "Let us not grow weary while doing good, for in due season we shall reap if we do not lose heart."

- 1 Corinthians 14:40 – "Let all things be done decently and in order."

- Psalm 128:1-4 – "Blessed is every one who fears the Lord, who walks in His ways…"

Closing Prayer

Father God,

Thank You for the precious gift of marriage. Thank You for joining us together in love and purpose. Lord, we ask You to help us continue to invest in this covenant with joy, humility, and wisdom. Show us where to give more, speak more, serve more, and love more. Help us to value one another as You value us.

Father, bring order to every area of our marriage—our hearts, our home, our finances, our intimacy, and our priorities. Let our relationship reflect Your glory and become a light to others around us.

We choose today to treasure this sacred union and to sow generously into it. Help us to walk daily in love, unity, forgiveness, and grace. Let our love grow deeper, stronger, and richer as we stay rooted in You.

We declare Colossians 1:9–14 over our marriage:

"Fill us with the knowledge of Your will in all wisdom and spiritual understanding… that we may walk worthy of You, fully pleasing You, being fruitful in every good work, and increasing in the knowledge of God…"

We receive Your blessing over our home and our future.

In Jesus' Name,

Amen.

About the Author

Pastor Candy LaFlora is a passionate teacher, worship leader, and author with a heart for strengthening marriages and drawing people into a deeper relationship with God. Alongside her husband, Pastor Stephen LaFlora, she co-pastors Maranatha Church in Chicago, where they have ministered together for over 30 years.

With a rich legacy of faith and love passed down from her parents, Pastor Chester and Beatrice Dickerson, Pastor Candy has dedicated her life to encouraging couples to walk in unity, purpose, and godly intimacy. Her life and ministry are marked by compassion, wisdom, and a joyful authenticity that uplifts every heart she reaches.

Through her books, music, and speaking ministry, she continues to equip others to live out the kind of love that endures, honors God, and brings lasting fruit.

To learn more or to connect,
visit www.stephenandcandy.com

Additional Books by Candy LaFlora

Who Is This Person That I Married – Have you ever woken up next to your spouse and silently wondered, "Who is this person that I married?" If so, you're not alone. Many couples—whether newlyweds or decades into marriage—have found themselves at a crossroads, questioning their relationship, their choices, and their connection.

In this transparent, heartfelt, and faith-filled book, Candy LaFlora explores the real, often unspoken moments of marriage that can leave even the strongest couples wondering if they truly knew what they signed up for. Through personal reflections, spiritual insight, and practical wisdom, she reminds us that marriage isn't for the faint of heart—it's for the grown folk, as one wise woman once said.

But there's hope. When God is the center of the union—when two mature individuals walk together with Him—marriage can become a beautiful dance of destiny and purpose. With honesty and grace, Candy shares how couples can regain their rhythm, find healing, and rediscover the person they once fell in love with.

Who Is This Person That I Married will challenge you to see your spouse through God's eyes, grow in emotional and spiritual maturity, and embrace the process of becoming one—through every season of love and life.

Whether you're preparing for marriage, navigating the challenges of your current relationship, or simply seeking to strengthen your bond, this book is a powerful reminder: when God is involved, no question is too big, and no relationship is beyond restoration.

Love Assignments – 21 Days to Rekindle the Flame in Your Marriage

Love Assignments is a 21-day challenge designed to spice up and strengthen your marriage—one simple, fun, and intentional step at a time. Whether you're newlyweds or have been together for decades, this interactive book offers creative daily assignments that inspire laughter, affection, and deeper connection.

Each day features a doable act of love that will help rekindle intimacy, restore joy, and remind you both why you fell in love in the first place. From heartfelt notes to lighthearted surprises, these assignments will breathe fresh life into your relationship.

Plus, you'll find a set of playful and exciting love coupons in the back of the book—perfect for surprising your spouse and keeping the flame alive long after the 21 days are over.

Let Love Assignments be your guide to making marriage fun again. Start the challenge today—and fall in love all over again.

Maximize Your Expectations – helps you to recognize your personal forecast for everything in your life, and how to change it if your outcomes have not been favorable. Often, we SAY we're expecting one thing while everything else about us says something else. Our core belief system becomes evident by what we say and what we do, thus revealing our true expectations. No worries! By the time you finish reading this book, your words and actions will be in perfect alignment with the blessed and meaningful life that God wants you to have.

Candy's Children's Book

- *I Love To Sing To Jesus* – a children's book inviting young ones into worship

- *I Love To Play For Jesus* – Brand New Release children's book celebrating music-making for God

This is your invitation to experience the joy, healing, and intimacy God intended for your marriage.

This book is for you.

For the couple that wants more.

For the spouse who feels unseen.

For the marriage that needs a fresh wind of hope.

Let this be the tool that brings new life, deeper understanding, and lasting intimacy to your relationship.

JeQuen Music & Publishing Inc
Stephen and Woola LaFlora Ministries
PO Box 205
Olympia Fields, IL 60461
708-506-7324
stephenandcandy.com

9 798990 052437